I0520689

The promise

L.T. Kenneth

Copyright © 2015 L.T. Kenneth

All rights reserved.

ISBN-13: 978-0-9922256-5-0

DEDICATION

Manthati Lehlosi and friends…

ACKNOWLEDGMENTS

Love is pure and peaceful, only two people can vouch.

PROLOGUE

Jasmine Reynolds is an editor at a high profiled magazine company in New York. She has worked hard for her position through the years to get where she is today. She wasn't born into money like a lot of her co-workers. She had to fight her way through school, working 3 jobs to keep up with her bills. She moved away from home when she was 16. She lived with friends and worked until she graduated high school. When she finally made it to college she had to work twice as hard. Money was tight back then. She got a partial scholarship which allowed her to get a small place near the campus. She finally graduated college and at the top of her class. She now has a job that she loves and she's good at. Now at 25 with a 7 year old will she be able to handle the curve-ball life throws at her? Will the past come back to haunt her?

L.T. Kenneth

CHAPTER 1

8 years earlier

"Jas you ready? The movie starts in an hour!"

Daniel yells.

God he is so bossy.

If he wasn't so cute I'd slap him.

Daniel Jones is the hottest Football Captain ever! Number 24 and he's all mine. It's our senior year and we have been dating for almost a year now. Everything is perfect. "Yea Danny geez give me a second to get shoes on!" I yell back. The theater is only 20 minutes away. What's the big rush? "I'm not sitting in the back row with all the little kids again Jas." Danny whines. I walk out of the bedroom and grab my jacket. Danny's standing there in his blue jeans and our high school hoodie. GO JACKSON HIGH. "I'm ready now king." I jokingly say. "Well thank god for that!" he laughs back at me. We head out the door to his mustang that's sitting in the driveway of my friend's house. This is where I'm currently living.   After my mom left me and my dad never really got along so it made more sense for me to move out. I have an awesome friend, Kylie with just as awesome parents. I work at a grocery store where Kylies' mom is a manager. It doesn't pay much but they don't charge me rent anyway. I'm saving what I do make for college which again her parents helped me apply for scholarships and opened me a savings account. I have a good bit saved since I baby sit on my off nights also.   "Jasss get in the car!" Danny yells. "OH MY GOD DANNY REALLY!!!! I'm walking around the damn car right now!" I yell back at him. This boy is impatient.   I jump in we buckle up and head to the theater. Once we arrive we meet up with some of Danny's' friends from the football team. They like to talk a lot. Danny has been talking about joining the marines like his dad was. He hasn't decided yet but it's a strong possibility. He always wanted to be like his dad. "Ready to go in?" I ask. He nods after doing the oddest handshakes I've ever seen. These guys are so weird. I just don't understand guy code I guess.

After the movie we all hang out at the local diner and eat. We are making plans to go out to the old train station. The train station is about a mile outside of our little town and there's a huge river that runs right behind it. "Who all's going out to the station?" I ask.   Allot of our friends speak up and say they are going. "I don't know if we should go out tonight Jas I really need to talk to my dad about the Marine paperwork." Danny says.   I know this has been on his mind a lot since we are so close to graduation but we need to have some fun time. "I know you do babe but let's go hang out for a while we won't stay late." I say.   He nods and we finish up at the diner and head out again. Once we make it to the station its like high schoolers gone wild! Everyone is running around yelling and laughing. I love having this time. It makes for the best memories. Spending time with my friends is important since we all are headed different directions after high school.   Some of us college, some not or like Danny and his friend Josh the Marine Corp. Everything's perfect. We are all having a good time and some people are drinking. Me and Kylie decide to go out on a limb and jump from the rocks across the lake. "Jas I don't think that's a good idea do you?" Danny asks. He's such a worrier. "Why not? It's not like we are the first ones to jump. It will be fine." I say back. "Yea but Jas the waters down a little." he argues. "Thanks dad I'll remember that when I jump." I joke with him. "Hey Josh come jump with us." I yell. Josh is Danny's best friend. They have been neighbors since they were 2. They do everything together. Football and the Marines are no different. Josh jumps up stumbling around he says, "Weellll I maybe a little drunk. But what the hell!" Of course Danny being the fatherly worry wart he chimes in "No no no Josh your very drunk sit your ass down. You can't even swim across there." With that being said a drunken Josh jumps in the water. "Well look at me I can dead man float across this shit." He spouts off. Me and Kylie take of our clothes down to our bra and underwear and jump in. Holy shit this water is cold! "Oh my godddd I'm freezing!" Kylie yells. "Josh aren't you cold?"   We look over at Josh as we start to swim across. "Nope but I wasn't too drunk to strip either." He yells back. We giggle and swim across the lake. As we reach the shore we climb out shivering and shaking. This wasn't a good idea. Why is it even so cold tonight? It's almost summer!   We wait on "Mr. Dead man float" to climb out of the water before we start to climb up the rocks. "Damn ladies mighty fine view from the back." He slurs.   We both cut our eyes at him and laugh.

Yea he's drunk alright.   We climbed up the tall rocks and stand by the edge. Me and Kylie both look down and back at each other. We have never done this before but we have seen a lot of our friends do it. Josh comes up behind us and asks us what we are waiting for. "You know its ladies first." He states.   Me and Kylie take one last look at each other and grab each other's hands. We count to 3 and jump. We hit the water and our hands break apart. We both resurface laughing like crazy people.   We swim out a little and hear Josh yell "Outta the way ladies, let a man show you how it's done!!"   A few seconds later Josh jumps. He makes a splash and we hear everyone back on shore cheering and laughing.   We wait. Josh hasn't come back up.   Where is he? We look around a little more and then we see him "dead man floating."   "Damn-it Josh you ass you scared us!" I yell.   He doesn't answer. Oh God. I hope he's playing. Me and Kylie start to swim towards him. Danny's yelling "What's he doing?"   We don't turn around we just swim. We make it over to where Josh is floating see blood on his head. OH MY GOD he wasn't playing. I grab him yelling his name over and over. No answer. "JOSHH JOSSHHH wake up." I'm screaming.   Danny is behind me now. I have no idea when he even got in the water. "Someone call 911." He screams calmer than I am. "You two get to the shore and get dressed I got him. HURRY!" He yells at me and Kylie. We do as we are told and as soon as he has Josh on the shore the ambulance shows up.

CHAPTER 2

We called Josh's' parents on the way to the hospital. They are supposed to be on their way but they were both at work over an hour away. Me and Danny and a few others sit in the waiting room at the hospital waiting to hear anything. It's been 30 minutes and we don't know anything. The police have been here asking questions about the drinking. Since we are all underage they will want to call all of our parents and let them know the situation. Lucky for me and Danny we weren't drinking but they still want to inform our parents. I guess I'm the lucky one since my dad doesn't care. We watch the clock tick by. Now it's been an hour. Josh's parents come rushing in with his little sister Jane. They come straight toward Danny. "Anything news? Have they said anything?" Mr. Whitmire screams. "No sir, we haven't heard anything." Danny says softly. Jane is crying so I go and take her hand. "He will be ok Jane. Your brothers a strong guy." I calmly say to her. She just nods. She's 6. What 6 year old would understand anyways? "Family of Mr. Whitmire," A tall manly doctor calls. Mr. and Mrs. Whitmire run over to the doctor and we all follow. "Would you folks like to go somewhere more private?" the doctor asks. "No" Mr. Whitmire says "These are his family also." He nods his head towards us. "Ok then. Well as you know your son had been drinking tonight and jumped off of some rocks. Apparently when he hit the water he also hit rock underwater. Now he does have a very large cut on his head which we did stitch up but he is in a coma as of right now. He also has some broken vertebrae. Meaning his back is broken. Mr. and Mrs. Whitmire I hate to say this but there is a chance that Josh will be paralyzed from the neck down. This is a wait and see game now. First we need to wait and see if and when he comes out of the coma. Only then will we know about the rest. I'm very sorry." Mrs. Whitmire drops to the floor in tears and screams. Mr. Whitmire falls behind her. Danny looks at me and begins to cry. I go to him and hug him. Letting all his pain seep into me. This is his best friend. They have never been apart. "Let's go. I need to be alone with Jas. Please let's get out of here." He cries. I nod and take his hand leading him out of the hospital.

CHAPTER 3

"Where do you want to go Danny?" I ask quietly. He chokes on a sob and says "let's just go to the football field." We drive in silence. Well all but the sobs I hear coming from Danny as we drive toward the school. Once we get there I park the car and we get out and walk around a little. Danny's quite. So I just walk in the quietness of the night with him. I grab his hand and we just walk the field. I don't know how long we walk but its awhile. Danny's phone ringing breaks the silence. "Hello?" Danny answers. "Ok thanks for calling. Ill check in tomorrow. I'm sorry Mrs. Whitmire. Bye." Danny stands still for a few minutes when he finally looks down at me. "There's no change. Doctor says we just have to keep waiting." He says. "I'm so sorry Danny. He will be ok." I say calmly. He starts walking again and I catch up to him. I start to talk when Danny cuts me off. "Jas I just need to be with you right now." He says. I nod and he grabs me and kisses me. If that's what Danny needs I will give him anything he wants. I love him. There's

no doubt in my mind that he loves me too.
We lay together tangled in each other's naked
bodies for hours. It's a bitter sweet feeling. I
can't help but think that this is all my fault. If
we didn't go and I didn't ask Josh to jump with
us. It's a sickening feeling. "Danny I'm sorry. I
feel like this is my fault. I shouldn't have asked
him to jump." I say quietly. I lay there for a
few minutes and Danny never responds. I start
to say something else and I hear him. He's
crying again. I hate the feeling I have when he
cries. There's nothing I can do. I have ruined
not one but two lives tonight. Why did I even
have to go?

CHAPTER 4

Weeks pass and Josh is still the same. It's
coming up on graduation in a few days. We all
went to school and finished out the year like
zombies. No one really talks anymore. Kylie is
so quite these days it's hard to tell we even live
in the same house. I try to stay busy at work or
babysitting to keep my mind off things. It's
hard. Danny barely speaks to me or anyone for
that matter. He keeps to himself which is so
unlike him. Every day I try to talk to him but he
just blows me off with another excuse. I can't

handle anymore. I have to talk to him. We haven't talked about the Marines or college. I don't even know if he plains on going now. I decide I'm going to talk to him today whether he likes it or not. I'm deep in thought about what to say and how to say it when he walks through the door.   He looks at me with a terrible look on his face like he wants to be sick. Oh no. Did something happen with Josh? Is he ok? "Danny can we talk?" I ask. He turns and stares at me. I wait. "Yea but we got to make it fast. I want to get back up to the hospital." He says dryly.   "Want to go out to the field? It will be quite there." I ask. He nods and we start to walk toward the doors. It's hot today. Today would have been a good swimming day but no one does much of that anymore.   We walk out onto the field and head towards the bleachers. I sit down on the first row and tug Danny's hand so he sits next to me. He doesn't pull away which is good. Right?   "Danny I think we need to talk about everything. We haven't talked in weeks. Have you decided what you're doing about the Marines?" I ask looking at him. He nods. He doesn't speak just nods. "Well?" I ask. He sits quietly for a minute. "Jas I can't do this anymore. I'm going to the Marines and well... I just can't do this." He says. What can't he do? Is he afraid of going? Of leaving Josh? Oh leaving me?   "Danny I will be fine. We will write letters and call when we can. Everything will be ok." I say matter of factly. At that Danny turns to me. "Jasmine, you don't get it. I can't write or call you. I can barely look at you!   I mean I can't do this with you Jasmine. Ever since the accident I just can't function. You just had to get him to jump didn't you? He was drunk and I told you the damn water was low. Why the hell didn't you listen to me Jas? HUH? Why couldn't you for once in your damn life listen to me?? My best friend... My brother may never wake up and if he is lucky enough to wake up he will never walk again! Do you have any idea what you did? You have destroyed him, his future, and his life! This is all your fault Jasmine!" He screams.   I sit there dumbfounded. Crying. Tears that won't stop. He believes it's all my fault. "I'm so sorry Danny. I truly am. If I had known I would have never jumped or asked him to jump." I choke out between the tears. "You know what Jasmine. Stop crying because you're alive. You're moving. You can walk and run and do everything in life you've ever wanted! You have never listened to me before but you damn sure better listen to me now. I don't want to be with you anymore. I don't want to see you ever again! I can't be with you

knowing you caused this!" He screams again.
And with that he gets up and walks away.

CHAPTER 5

Graduation was a disaster. No one
seemed happy. Josh didn't get to graduate with
his class. It was sweet though. They let his little
sister Jane except his diploma for him.
Everyone cheered for her and she cried the
whole time. It was nice to see the Whitmires
again. I haven't seen them since the hospital.
"Congratulations Jasmine. I wish Josh was here
with you guys. You are his best friends you
know." Mrs. Whitemire hugs me tightly and I
feel the tears start to flow. I can't speak. I just
nod. What can I say? I messed their lives up.
How can they even consider me his friend?
"Well well well Miss Jane how are you my fair
lady?" Danny calls as he walks over toward us.
She smiles up at Danny. She loves him to death
like her own brother. "Congratulations
Jasmine." He says to me. "Thanks Danny you
too." I say in return. He stands there staring at
me like I don't belong here. I feel the hatred
coming off him in waves and it's all directed at
me. Mrs. Whitmire seems to notice the tension
between us as she looks back and forth from
Danny to me but she doesn't say anything.

"Well I guess I need to get going. Please tell Josh and Mr. Whitmire "Hi" for me. It was nice seeing you both." I say to Mrs. Whitmire and Jane. "Nice seeing you too dear." Mrs. Whitmire says back. Jane smiles and waves. I start to say goodbye to Danny but he has already turned his back to me.

CHAPTER 6

"You have everything packed?" Kylie stands in the doorway of our bedroom we share at her house. I'm going to miss being here. "Yea I think so. You?" I ask. She nods. "Well mom and dad want to say goodbye to us and blah blah. You know how they are." Kylie makes mocking hand signals. I laugh and so does she. It's good to be laughing again. Me and Kylie got into the same college that's 4 hours away. We have already found a place to rent near campus and have some jobs setup. We are ready to go. I think we all need a new start. As much as I hate leaving without Danny there's really nothing I can do. Kylie grabs my hand and we head out into the living room to say our goodbyes to her parents. We round the living room corner and see Danny standing there. "Hi" he says. I let go of Kylies hand and walk over to him. "Hey" I reply. "Can we go outside and talk for a second Jas?" he asks quietly. I look over at Kylie's parents and they both nod. I have a few minutes. Wonder what this is about. I hope it's not to blame me anymore. I walk over to the front door and open it. We walk outside and sit on the front porch steps. Neither one of us saying anything. After a long silence Danny finally speaks. "I can't say I'm sorry Jas. I can't be with you. I can't help what I'm feeling." There's a long silence again. I don't know what exactly he has to say. Is there more? Hasn't he said enough? I sit with my hands in my lap twisting them around and around. This hurts. We have been together so long. I feel tears prickle my eyes. They start to fall before I can stop them. "Jas there's a part of me that will always love you. You know that. I just don't think I can get past this Jas. I don't know how to. "He says quietly. Not letting me reply or say a single word he stands up and walks away. There goes the only person I have ever loved. I ruined his life. I ruined his best friend who was like a brother. It was all my fault.

CHAPTER 7

"Kegger tonight??" Kylie is screaming

and dancing around. "Ummm HELL YEA!"
Is my reply. Wow was that even a question?
We have been in college now for 3 months. We
are having a blast. My classes are awesome.
Living off campus is the best since we can have
some pretty wild parties and not have to worry
about the on campus security showing up. We
have had a few good parties here. Tonight we
are hitting a sorority party. From what we have
heard these are the best. There weren't a lot of
them at first but now that everyone is settled in
to the college life they are everywhere. "Wear
that new dress you just bought, you know the
skanky one." I tell Kylie. "Skanky? My dress is
not skanky! It's just lacking fabric is all." She
states with a fake mad face. I start laughing and
so does she. "Well you can explain that to all
the guys that will be falling all over that lack of
fabric later." I laugh and say back to her. She
just smiles and nods on her way to get ready. I
start to get ready when my phone rings. "Hello"
I answer without looking at the screen. "Hey
Jas." I hear the voice of the last person I
thought I'd be hearing. Danny. Shocked I say
"Danny? Hey How are you?"   There's silence
for a second and I think he has hung up.
"Danny?" I say. "Yea Jas I'm here. I uh. I don't
even know why I'm calling you but uh Jasmine,

Josh died last night. His parents decided to take him off the machines and he just couldn't do it on his own." I hear Danny start to cry. "Danny I'm so sorry." I say. "Look Jasmine I didn't call you for that. I called because I have to leave tomorrow to go to training. I don't have a choice. The funeral is Monday at 3pm. I was uh shit, I was just going to see if you could go and be there for his parents and sister. Even if they don't know everything that happened that night they love you Jas and need you there. Do you think you can make it?" He says. Wow he still isn't over it. It's been months. This is the first time he has talked to me since graduation. I miss him. "Danny I miss you. When you're ready to talk I'm still here you know?" I ask quietly. I hear him sigh long and hard. " Jas I miss you too. You have no idea how hard this is for me. I just don't know how to get past this. I don't know if I can." he says it like he means it. I don't want to except that it's really over. I have given him time and I will give him more if that's what he needs. "I'll be there Danny. Thanks for calling me."I say softly. I wait for a reply but all I hear are sobs and then the line goes dead.

CHAPTER 8

"It was a lovely funeral Mrs. Whitmire." I say hugging her after the service. "Thanks for being here sweetie. I know how much it would mean to Josh that you were here. It's been hard on us all." She says sweetly. The funeral was lovely. His casket was white with gold trim. His football buddies all signed a ball and put in with him along with a mini helmet. Mrs. Whitmire knew how much football meant to him so he was buried in his varsity jacket. It was hard seeing him lying there knowing that was the end. The last time we would ever see him again. I felt bad for Danny for having to miss it but I also knew Josh would understand. As I'm starting to walk toward the exit a wave of nausea hits me and I run toward the bathroom. Great now I'm going to be sick. I knew I should have eaten this morning before we left the house.   As soon as I come out of the bathroom I hear "Where did you run off to? Some hot guy in the bathroom?" Kylie says with a half-smile as she glances around me toward the bathroom. "Really Kylie at a funeral? I am not that freaky!" I say back to her. She flashes me a smile and says "Yea well have you seen the guys? Damn how did they grow up that much in a few months?"   Oh this girl is a mess. A few of the guys had asked her out back in high school and she always turned them down. Now she is drooling all over herself looking at them. "Wow Kylie you really have issues girl!" I laugh and swat at her. "Let's go get something to eat I'm starving." I say.

CHAPTER 9

We drive past my old house before heading out of town. Dads old Buick is sitting in the driveway. I think about stopping by just to see how he is but decide against it. After the funeral I'm not really in the mood to hear about what a failure I am. Sometimes I miss the old house but I quickly hear the words out of dad's mouth and I'm over it. We head back toward the college and decide to stop at a diner on the way out of town. "Jas lets go shopping." Kylie smiles "I'm too depressed to go home yet." "I'm pretty sure you aren't depressed when I just seen you checking that guy out!" I laugh back at her. She is so crazy. She will say anything to go shopping. "Fine flirty. Let's go shopping." I smile back at her. We walk across the street after we finish eating and Kylie is headed straight to the sporting goods store. I give her an awkward look and then just laugh. I know what she's doing. Those guys just went in here. "Really Kylie? What exactly are you going to do in there? "I question her pointing at the store. "Well first I am going to get a good look at those hot guys and then I may need a new pair of running shoes." She smiles back at me. "Kylie you don't run." I laugh as we head into the store. "So maybe I'm going to start and I can't start without good shoes." She defends herself playfully.   We go in the store and this girl has gone all commando on me. She's peeking through the clothes racks and under the shelves. All I can do is laugh which gets me some pretty unfriendly looks from Kylie. God I love this girl. "Shut Up Jas and come here."She whispers. "Kylie Rayne I am drawing the line at getting on the floor to stalk some man!" I say back to her. Has this girl truly lost her mind? "Hi" A male voice says behind me. I spin around to see a tall good looking guy standing there. He's cute with his pretty blue eyes and blonde shaggy hair. "Hey" I say back as Kylie pays no attention to me and is still on the floor. "I can't see them now "she huffs as another guy is smiling like a crazy person drops to the floor behind her and says "Damn now what are we going to look at?" He whispers.   Kylie jumps off the floor hitting her head on the clothes rack making the rest of us die of laughter. "Oh dang Umm.. Yea so... Hi." She tries to play it off. "So what exactly were we looking at down there?" The guy asks her. "YOU! The girl has been staking you since we came in here!" I blurt out in a fit of laughs. "JASMINE!!!" she yells. I can't help but laugh even more. The girl has lost her mind. "I'm Jackson and this is my friend Cole." The guy introduces himself to us. "I'm Jasmine and that stalker there is Kylie. Nice to meet you guys." I say with a smile. "Well Kylie and Jasmine we were just going to head to the fair care to meet us over there?" Jackson asks. "YES, umm Yea yea we were thinking about going to." Kylie says without letting him finish. They both laugh and nod. "Ok so we will meet you guys over there." Cole says.

CHAPTER 10

We drive the short ways to the fair and hang out with the guys. It was pretty fun. They are totally nice and we even found out they go to our school and were just out checking out the nearby towns to see what all they had going on. We all exchange numbers and decided we would hang out the next weekend. Before we make it back to the house I get a text from Cole. "Hey, wanted to make sure you guys made it home ok. And wanted to see if you wanted to get dinner later? I had fun talking to you and want to get to know you." Kylie's jumping out of her seat yelling at me that I better go! It's only dinner. I'm not looking for anything else. I still can't be over Danny so I guess making new friends is ok. I text back. "Sure pick me up? 612 Risen St." I wait a few mines and get a text back. "Yep I'll be there at 6. TTYL" Well that was easy. "You think I should call Jackson? "Kylie chimes in. "Yea why not?" I say back to her. She does and they agree to meet up later too. We go home and hang out awhile and get ready to go. Right at 6 Cole shows up. We go out to eat and hang out walking around town awhile. It's nice he is a really nice guy. We decide to call it a night and we get in the car to head back to the house. "We should hang out again sometime." Cole says. "Yea that would be great." I say back to him. He smiles as we pull through the intersection. Out of nowhere a truck slams into the side of Cole's car. "Jasmine are you ok?? " Cole yells. "I think so; I think I'm going to be sick." I say as I begin to throw up. After Cole makes sure the other driver is ok he comes back to sit next to me on the curb as we wait on the police and ambulance. "I called Jackson and Kylie they are going to meet us at the hospital."

He says rubbing my back. "I don't need to go to the hospital I'm fine." I say. "No you're not your throwing up and you have a cut on your head. It probably needs stitches Jasmine." He says back.   I didn't even know I had a cut on my head. I reach up to touch it and wow that hurt.   I agree to go just to keep Cole happy. Every time I said No he got aggravated so I gave in. Once we arrived at the hospital they take Cole to a different room to check his arm. The doctor comes in to look at my head and says I will need a few stitches and they were doing some blood work as a routine thing. 45 Minutes later my head is stitched up and I'm sitting on the bed waiting to be released. knock knock. I hear someone at the door. It pushes open a little bit and I see Cole peek in. "Hey Jasmine can I come in?" He says quietly. "Yea come on. You ok?" I ask. He comes in and I notice his arm is in a sling. "Oh no your arm!" I gasp. "Its fine just sprained is all. I see you got them stitches." He says with a half-smile. I smile back. We sit talking for a few minutes when the doctor comes back in. "Jasmine, I got your blood work back and everything looks good. I'd like to get an ultrasound to check on the baby though." He says plainly. Baby? What baby? He must have the wrong chart. Cole looks at me with the same "What the heck" look I have. "Umm I think you may have the wrong chart or something because I'm not pregnant." I state matter of factly. Looking through the chart he simply says "If you didn't know you were pregnant than congratulations you two. The nurse will be in in a few minutes to the ultrasound." I sit there dumbfounded. I can't be. Can I? Me and Danny aren't even speaking. He wants nothing to do with me. I can't be. Cole steps out of the room to go get Kylie. We both sit in silence while the nurse does the ultrasound. "There's the heartbeat right there." She smiles. Me and Kylie look at a little flashing blob on the screen. That is a heartbeat? My baby's heartbeat. "You are about 3 months according to this. Congratulations." The nurse finishes up.

CHAPTER 11

The months go by quickly and before I know it I'm already 8 months pregnant. Kylie has been awesome to me and Cole has been a great friend. Anything I need he's been there. I wasn't ready for a relationship before I knew and I sure am not ready for one now. Cole has been sweet about everything. He has asked me a million times to be with him but I can't. We are still in college. We both have things we want to do and become in life. I can't put my problems off on him that's just wrong and I won't do it. Never the less he has been around the whole time. "Have you called Danny yet?" Cole asks as we sit and watch a movie. He really thinks I should but from what Kylie has talked to her parents he is in training and can't be reached anyway. "No I haven't and I don't think I am. He doesn't want anything to do with me and I don't need him anyway." I say back quietly. "He has a right to know Jas." He says back. "Look I have a lot of work to do." I say back quickly. He takes that as his queue to leave. He stands up and kissed my forehead and leaves. I do have a lot to do. I'm enroling in online courses after I have the baby but I am cramming as much work in as I can ahead of time. I want to be able to keep up so I have been working on extra stuff to get ahead. I will not be a college drop out. I've come too far and I want to do something with my life. Now that I have another life to take care of I have to finish what I started. I push myself extra hard knowing that.

CHAPTER 12

3 years later

"Kegan come on we have to go now. Get teddy

and come on." I yell to my son. I know I can't believe it. My son. 3 years old he is the spitting image of his daddy. I finished college online and was able to graduate a little early. I also got an amazing job offer in New York! I couldn't believe it. All my dreams are coming true. Sure it was rough trying to juggle school, work and being a mom but I'm no quitter. I made it happen and now we are getting all packed up to move. "Momma I can't find him!" Kegan cries. "Come on bud Aunt Kylie will help you find him ok?" I hear Kylie say to him. She is the best. I'm really going to miss her. ALOT. Kylie is moving back home with her parents for a while. Her mom quit working to take care of her grandmother and Kylie wants to be close to home. She got a job at her father's law firm. She is a paralegal. Her dad took her on immediately. I know it wasn't her first choice but she wants to be near her family so I understand that. "Momma I go him I got him." Kegan runs and jumps into my arms. He is the light of my life. "Come on babe we need to get going it's a long drive." Cole says. Cole and I have been engaged for a year now. He has always been my rock the last few years. He has never left my side and has never been anything but encouraging. Once he heard about my job offer he decided he was going to New York with us. It was never much of a question to him. He wants to be wherever we are. He went to school to become a lawyer so he can work anywhere. He went to New York early to take the bar there and he passed without an issue. He also got us an apartment set up while he was there. I'm glad I have him. "I know I say just give me a second with Kylie please." I say almost in tears. He nods. "Come on my little man let's get you in the car so mommy can have girl time. " He takes Kegan from me and hugs him. "Eww gross girl time." Kegan giggles. Kylie walks around the corner "Hey now I'm a girl and your favorite aunt." She teases him. He giggles away as Cole puts him in his car seat. I grab Kylie in a big bear hug. "What am I going to do without you?" I cry. She has been my everything since we were kids. We have been together every day. I don't know how to live without her. "You're going to go to work and make a beautiful life with your sweet baby and Cole. You are strong Jas, you always have been. You will make and it and we will visit. We will talk every day!" She says sounding so sure about everything. That's Kylie. Always positive. We hug and cry and hugs some more. Now it's time to go.

CHAPTER 13

5 years later

I can't believe it's been 5 years since we have moved to New York. Time really flies here. I love my job and I love Cole. We still haven't gotten married yet. We are still engaged. I don't know why Cole hasn't set a date for us to get married. He says it's because he wants us to be completely settled first. We have been here for 5 years I figured we were settled. Kegan loves his school and is a really smart kid. He is the best thing that ever happened to me. Like Kylie promised we talk all the time. I haven't been back to Texas to visit but she has made a few trips here. She makes sure to come for Kegan's birthday every year and Christmas. She doesn't have to be here to spoil that boy rotten. I swear every time we come home there's another package waiting for him. She makes sure he knows he is loved by her too.

CHAPTER 14

"Is that report ready yet?" I say to Chase, a man that works for me. "On your desk boss." He says. I walk through the office feeling great.

It's a great day and everyone is moving along today. "Thanks Chase. Have you seen Jenna?" I ask. "Earlier she said she left messages on your desk, a few are Rushed." Chase says quickly before turning to go back to work. I go into my office and I'm greeted by a vase of flowers. I smile the biggest smile and grab the card after I smell the roses. I open the little card. "

"Jas, Just because I love you Cole"

He is the best. I smile at the card and text him a thank you. I know he's busy right now so I don't call. I start to go through my messages mostly work related then one hits me. I pick it up and read over the note. It's from a home health agency in Texas. That's weird. Wonder what that's about. I pick up the paper and dial the number. "Texas home health can I help you?" The voice on the other end says. "Yes my name is Jasmine Reynolds I had a message to return your call." I say. I hear paper riffling around. "Yes Miss Reynolds I was calling about your father. Mr. Reynolds is no longer able to be on our services and we wanted to see if we needed to set up an appointment for hospice?" She says. I sit there not knowing what to say. I don't know what's going on. "Ma'am I'm not sure what it is you're talking about. I haven't spoken to my father in years." I say confused. "Miss Reynolds we had your name as next of kin for your father. We had some people check around and found you in New York. Your father has cancer. It's in its final stages right now Miss Reynolds which takes him from our services to hospice." She explains. Cancer. She said cancer. Why did no one try to contact me until now? This is crazy. "Miss Reynolds? Are you there?" She says breaking my train of thought. "Yes I'm sorry I'm here. Yes please get with hospice. I will be returning to Texas as soon as I can." I say as calmly as I can. I hang up the phone and call Cole. He answers and I tell him what's going on. He can't leave I knew that so I explain to him that me and Kegan are going to fly back tonight and get everything in order. He agrees and I call Kylie to let her know what was going on and she agrees to pick us up at the airport.   I pick Kegan up from school and explain everything to him. He knows about his grandfather and that we didn't speak anymore. He didn't ask questions. He was 8 years old. He didn't know about cancer. We quickly pack and head out to the airport.

CHAPTER 15

"Aunt Kylieeeeee." Kegan is running and yelling. He hugs her without knocking her over which is good.   They hug and hug and smile. "I've missed you bud." she says to him. "Hey girly how are you doing?" She says to me. I shrug. What can I do?   We head out of the airport and head toward our hometown. We chat and catch up on the way there. Kegan's mouth hasn't stopped since we got in the car. We pull up to Kylie's house which is a few houses down from her parents. "I'll keep Kegan and you can take the car and handle things." She states. "Thanks Kylie. For everything." I say with a small smile.   I kiss Kegan by and head over to my dad's house where the hospice is meeting me. I pull up and I feel sick. The last time I was in this house I was 16 years old. I was being told how much of a failure I was. I walk up the front steps unaware of what I'll find or have to deal with. The hospice people are already here. We talk awhile about his health and what they can do to help make him comfortable. They tell me he doesn't have long left now. Maybe a few days. I walk down the hallway to my dad's bedroom. This house looks exactly the way it did the day I left.   His door is opened and I walk in. He looks terrible. If I was anyone else I'd be crying right now but I can't seem to let them flow. "Dad" I say as I walk up to the bed. He's thin. Very thin. He looks terrible not like the man I left here. "Your here." He states not sounding too happy about me being here. "Why are you here?" he says dryly. I told him how they agency had contacted me and filled me in on what was going on. I told him I would stay with him as long as he needed me to. I also told him about Kegan and asked if he would like to meet him. His response tore my heart out. "I don't need you here. I don't need to meet your bastard child either. IS that why you ran off from here? Because you wanted to go out make more mistakes? You wanted to become a bigger failure? Now you bring another failure into the world. Get out of my house you are not welcome here." He spits at me. That's it. It's one thing to talk to me that way but not about my son. I don't give him the satisfaction of an answer. I don't let him see me cry. I turn and walk back down the hallway and fill in the nurses that they may contact me for anything that I will be in town until the end. I will take care of his funeral and everything. I made sure to tell them to keep him as comfortable as possible and to call me with any changes. With that I turn and walk out the front door.

I'm crying. I'm crying hard by the time I reach the driveway. Why is he so evil? What did I ever do to him? Why wouldn't he at least want to meet his grandson before he was gone? The more I cry the more I think and I know I can't drive like this. I decide to take a walk instead. Crying and thinking I'm not even watching where I'm going and slam right into someone. Great that's what I need. Without looking up I say "I'm sorry excuse me." As I start to walk around the poor person I slammed into I hear a voice say. "Jasmine?" Oh my god. It can't be. I turn around and through my teary puffy eyes I look up and it's him. Daniel. I stand there and stare as if I've seen a ghost. He looks the same way at me but quickly puts a big smile on his face, "Jas wow. How are you? What are you doing here?" He asks questions quickly. "I....Uh ....." I begin to say but he cuts me off. "What's wrong Jas? You ok? You're crying." He says like he cares. "I'm fine. I mean I'm not. Everything's fine. I ... Uh .. Sorry I ran into like that I should have been watching where I was going." I say quickly. Why is he here? Why didn't Kylie tell me he was here? I start to turn around and walk back toward my dad's house to get the car when Danny stops me. "Something's wrong Jas. What's going on?" He asks like he cares. I haven't seen him in years why does he care now? "Everything's fine Daniel. I have to go." I say and quickly walk away.

CHAPTER 16

I head into Kylies house and she jumps and runs towards me. "We need to talk outside Jas ok?" She smiles and nods toward the door. We walk outside and quickly gives me a rundown of what I missed when I was out. Apparently Danny just got back in town and was making his way around to talk to everyone. He was going to my dad's to see if he has spoken to me. He went to Kylies parents too and they informed him that I was happily engaged and was living in New York. They didn't bring up Kegan which I am thankful for. I told her about my run in with him also. I also told her about what was going on with my dad. "Oh honey I'm so sorry. You're the best and you know it don't let him get you down." she says sweetly to me.   I take a break and call Cole and fill him in on what's going on. He has a lot of work to do so we don't talk long. I knew he would be busy but I just wanted to hear his voice. We spend the rest of the week hiding out I'm Kylies house. On Wednesday I got the call that my father had passed away. I quickly made the funeral arrangements. The funeral would be Friday morning.

CHAPTER 17

My dad didn't have many friends but as we stood graveside Friday morning a few people came by to pay their respects. Me, Kylie and Kegan stood there talking about him awhile. I didn't want Kegan to totally hate his grandfather so we told a few good stories from when we were younger. It seemed to keep Kegan's questions under control. Kylie had to get back to work so she left. Me and Kegan stood a little while longer. We were turning to walk to the car when I see him off in the distance. Daniel. Great this is not what I need now. He starts walking over to us and I notice a limp that I hadn't a week ago. Then again I wasn't really paying attention. "I'm really sorry about your dad Jas." He says. "Thanks Daniel. You know we weren't that close." I say back. "Mom can we get something to eat? I'm dying here." Kegan is whining. "Yes we will go get something to eat in a minute. Why don't you start heading to the car I'll be there in a second." I say back to him. I look over at him as he starts to walk back to the car and then look back at Daniel who has a shocked look on his face. "Mom? You have a son? He's yours?" Danny asks me shocked. I nod my head at him not meeting his eyes. "Jas?" he says a little louder. "How old is your son? And why the hell does he look just like me!?" He's yelling now. I close my eyes and rub them with my hands. This is so not good.

CHAPTER 18

"JASMINE ANSWER ME" he's in my face now. I look up at his confused face. "Calm down Daniel." I say. "No you answer me. How old is he?" he asks again a little quieter this time. "If you don't tell me I'll go ask him myself damnit!" That's it he hit a nerve. Now it's my turn to yell. "Damnit Daniel you will not go ask him anything. You have no right to ask him anything." I scream at him. "Then you tell me Jasmine and you tell me now!" He snaps back. "He's 8 Daniel, Kegan is 8 years old." I say softly. We stand there for a few seconds. Danny doesn't say anything. He just looks like he's doing the math. I start to walk away and he grabs my arm. "He's mine isn't he?" He asks quietly. I take a deep breath and sigh. "Yes Daniel he's yours." I say. "Does he know? Does he know I'm his dad? I am his dad. "He says. I take another deep breath. What do I say? What am I supposed to do now? I have to just be honest. "No he doesn't know. He knows he doesn't belong to Cole but he doesn't know about you either." I say.."Who's Cole?" he asks. "My fiancé." I reply. The silence grows and I can't handle it anymore. It's my turn to walk away.

CHAPTER 19

Me and Kegan go grab something to eat and head back to Kylies house. I promised Kegan we would stay a few more days so he can go the fair that's being set up. He has never been and I think he would enjoy it. I know I need to talk to him but I need to talk with Daniel again first. I ask Kylie if she knows where he might be staying and if she could keep Kegan while I go talk to him. She agrees like I knew she would. So I head out to see if I can find him. I went to his parents' house and they said he had just left. We had a nice chat. They informed me that he had been shot while he was in the marines and he was discharged because of it. They also told me he had some pretty bad PTSD after he came back. We talked a little longer and I gave them my cell number in case he came back before I found him. I walked away and kept walking. I ended up at the local park. There were kids running all over. We used to hang out at this park. It still looks exactly the same. "I'm sorry I yelled at you." I hear Daniels voice come from behind me where I sit on a swing. "It's fine . I should have told you a long time ago Danny. I just didn't think you'd want any of this. And I didn't want to mess up your plans." I say quietly without turning around. I feel his hands on my back. He starts to slowly push me on the swing. I just swing for a while. When the swing slows down Danny is sitting in the swing next to me. "Is he happy?" His voice is sad. "Very happy. He's a great kid. Loves football just like you. " I reply. He grabs my swing and pulls it to his. "I want to know him Jas. I want the chance. I miss you. I always have." He says in my ear. I shiver. I know I shouldn't but I have always missed Danny. He was everything to me and now I walk around every day with a little piece of him. "I want you to know him. He's perfect. But we are going to be headed back to New York in a few days so we will need to talk about visiting and things." I say quietly. Danny sits very still for a second before speaking again, " Jas do you love him?"   Where did that come from? Why is he asking me this?

"Yes I do love Cole." I say. "Do you love him more than me?" He asks quietly. What did he just say to me? He left me a long time ago. "Excuse me? Did you really just ask me that Daniel? You left me remember? You blamed me for Josh." I spit back at him. He flinches at my words. Yea let that sink in. He did this to me. How can he even ask me that after all these years? "Do you love me Jas?"He asks again. "Daniel I will always love you. You gave me a beautiful little boy. I'll always love you for that but Cole is my life now. You ruined what we had a long time ago. I don't even understand how you can ask me that." I say dryly back to him. "Jas I asked because I love you. I always have. I haven't gone a day without thinking about you and how much I missed you." He says. I quickly put my hand up and cut him off. Where does he get off saying this stuff to me? I stand and start to walk away.

"Jasmine don't walk away from me." He yells. I stop and turn around. "What Daniel? What do you want from me? HUH? What do you want?" I scream back. I'm going to lose it. I feel the tears prickle in my eyes. "A chance Jas. I want a new chance. I want you. I want my son. I want us. Before I was discharged I was shot a few times and I thought I was going to die. All I could think was how horrible I was to you. The things I said to you, how I treated you all the things I couldn't take back Jas. I thought I was dying and all I cared about was you. I wrote you letters every day that I was deployed. I never sent any because I didn't want to interrupt your life. I didn't know how to reach you either but I saved every one of them. You don't understand Jas how much you really mean to me." He starts to cry. I'm already crying. Can I do this? Can we go back and try to make things ok between us? But how? I have Cole. I have a life in New York. I can't do this. "I'm taking Kegan to the fair when it opens. Why don't you come with us and we will talk. We can tell him then. Just please give me some time to figure out how to tell him. Please?" I ask quietly. With a slight smile on his face he nods.

CHAPTER 20

I tried calling Cole last night and he never picked up. He must have been busy, I'm sitting on the couch watching TV when I hear someone knocking on the door. Kegan's out shopping with Kylie so I get up to answer the door. It's Daniel. "Hey can we talk a minute?" He asks. I nod and come out onto the porch. "I just wanted to say I'm sorry Jas I am. I been thinking and I really want to make things right." He says. Before I have a chance to reply a taxi pulls up in front of us. The door opens. It's Cole. I jump off the porch and run to him. He lifts me easily and hugs me. "What are you doing here?" I ask. "I talked to Kylie last night. She told me you were going to tell Daniel and Kegan. Look Jas I love you. You know I do but you don't love me." I start to say something and he cuts me off. "I know you love me Jas just not the way you love him." He looks toward Daniel. "I wouldn't get married because I knew Jas, I knew you loved him more. " I stand there tears running down my face. He wipes the tears and walks around me toward Daniel. Daniel stands. Oh no what's going on? What's he going to do?   Cole extends his hand to Daniel." I'm Cole." he says. Daniel grabs his hand. "I'm Daniel." he says. "I know who you are. I know you once hurt her. I know it destroyed her. I have been with her for years. I was there when she had your son and when she needed a friend. I love her so much but I know and always have known that her heart was with you. Kegan's a good kid. He always has been. I'm man enough to step back and let what happens happen. I know where he heart is and it has never been with me." Cole says confidently to Daniel. I cry harder. Cole grabs me and pulls me to him. Hugging me he continues, "She will always mean something to me as will Kegan but I can't get in the way of her heart. She means more to me than to do that. But I can tell you that if she gives you that second chance and you mess it up. I will be the one picking up your pieces for a second time." I can't speak. I just cry into Cole's shirt. He loves me enough to give me this chance. "You're a good man Cole. I hope she gives me that chance too. But even if she doesn't I want to be a father to my son. I can't thank you enough for being the man I wasn't a long time ago and keeping her safe and happy." Daniel says to him. That only makes me cry harder. Me and Cole say our goodbyes and I thank him. I do love him but he's right my heart has always been with Daniel. With that Cole leaves.

CHAPTER 21

"Mom hurry up I want to ride every single ride there." Kegan is yelling at me. "Kegan we have all night calm down." I say back. Kegan has never been to a real fair. He's seen them on TV before but in New York there's really not any fairs. He is so excited and I'm excited for him. We all head to the car and load up. Kylie is as excited as Kegan and can't sit still all the way there. Once we arrive we park and start heading toward the entrance. "Hey Jes. Kylie." Danny greets us. "Hey" we both say at the same time. "Mom really? Can't you people talk later there's rides in there!" Kegan complains. Wow I have never seen him so excited. It makes me smile. "Kegan don't be a brat. I want you to meet someone. Kegan this is my friend Danny." I say smiling. Danny puts his hand out to Kegan and He shakes it. "Nice to meet you Kegan." Danny says. "Nice to meet you too. Do you like rides? Have you been on them? I want to go on every one of them but moms too scared" Kegan says with a funny look on his face. "Well then I guess it's going to be a boy's day huh? Because I love these rides!" Danny says. Kegan jumps in the air yelling yea!!   He's super excited now. We head into the fair and the boys are off. Me and Kylie follow along behind them and talk as they go on every ride there is. "What are you thinking girly?" Kylie asks eyeing me. "I don't know what to think. Everything just feels normal and I think I like it." I reply honestly. She nods and we continue walking. The boys are screaming and yelling on the rollercoaster. It feels good to see Kegan so happy and he is so comfortable with Danny. Maybe breaking the news to him will be easier than I thought.   The boys walk up to us after they are off the rollercoaster all smiles. "Mom did you see us on there? That was awesome MOM you should go on it." Kegan says happily.   "OH MOM look can I play the football toss?" He screams. I nod and he runs off Kylie following him. "Your right Jas, he's great." Danny says. I nod and watch as Kylie tries to play the football toss not having much luck since Kegan is laughing like crazy. "I don't know what you think Jas but I really do want to be a dad if you will let me." Danny says softly. "I know you do and trust me I want you to be, it's just I have a job in New York and my life is there. I just don't know how to make it work." I reply. And that's the truth. I don't know how to make it work. I don't know what to do. "Danny come check this out." Kegan yells. Danny looks over at me and I smile and nod. Danny stops and kisses my forehead and then runs to Kegan. Why does this feel so right?

"You play football Kegan?" Danny asks. "Oh yea man I'm the best ever!!!" Kegan yells. I laugh and so does Kylie. The boy does have a way with words. "Well I might not be better than you but almost." Kegan says. Danny gives

me a strange look and I shrug. I have no idea
what he's talking about. "How did you know I
played Kegan?" Danny asks. "I found some
pictures and papers about you once in mom's
room. Sorry mom I was looking for paper and
seen them." Kegan says honestly. Danny gives
me a half smile. Yes I kept some old pictures
and articles on him. I had planned on one day
telling Kegan about his dad. Or at least I
thought I would. The boys go back to their
game. We have been here almost 4 hours. They
have been on every ride here and played every
game there is. Of course the duo won all kids
of prizes. They must have eaten 6 funnel cakes
each! Hope no one gets sick later. We decide it's
time to go and Kylie says she will catch up to us
later. We decide to take Kegan over to the park
so we can talk.   We all walk and the boys
continue their endless chatting. I walk behind
them and smile as I watch them. I catch a
glimpse of Danny smiling back at me too.
"Let's go sit over there by the lake." Danny says
and Kegan eagerly follows. "You know me and
your mom used to go swimming here when we
were younger?" Danny says to Kegan. "You
mean my mom had fun before?" He laughs.
"Hey now I have fun all the time!" I swat at
Kegan. "No you don't mom, you always seem
sad." Kegan says back. I guess he notices a lot

more than I thought. Danny just looks at me with a sad face. "Ok well enough of that, Kegan we have something we need to talk to you about." I say. "Well I need to say. Kegan you know Cole is not your real dad right?" I say to him. He nods his head yes. "Well Kegan, Danny is your dad. We had problems along time ago and that's why he hasn't been around." I say. Danny sits silent. He doesn't know what to say. Neither do I. "So you're my dad?" Kegan looks at Danny. "Yea Bud I am. And I know I haven't been around for you but that's going to change." Danny says back to Kegan looking nervous. Kegan looks back and forth between us and finally speaks. "Well, that's pretty awesome!! I mean you are cool and stuff and we like the same stuff." Kegan is smiling. "So does that mean you are moving to New York with us or are we moving here?" Kegan asks Danny. We look at each other unsure of what to say. We haven't talked about those things yet. "I mean cause I kind of like it here anyways" Kegan adds. Danny smiles a big smile at him and says "Well bud we will get that all figured out but for right now let's just hang out while we can. How about that?"   I can't help the smile on my face.

CHAPTER 22

6 months later

so here we are. We moved from New York into my dad's old house. He left it to me in his will. It took me off guard when the lawyer called me and told me. At first I thought he had lost his mind. I transferred for my job to a new company nearby. It doesn't pay as well but I get a lot of time to work from home which means more time with Kegan. Kegan has adjusted well to the move. He really likes the country small town feel here. He has made a lot of friends and is on the junior varsity football team. His dad is the new head coach of the team. Danny decided that since we were moving back home that he was going to stay too. We have all been spending a lot of time together. He is trying to be the best dad he can be and I must say he is doing a damn good job. He keeps talking about us getting married but he hasn't asked me yet. He has been going to counseling for his PTSD which scares me at times. He has had a rough time with everything going on. He has made a big improvement and I'm proud of him. Tonight is the last game of the football season and me and Kylie are sitting in the stands cheering them on.   Once the game has ended and most of the people are leaving I see Kegan standing in the middle of the field smiling like he won a prize. I look at Kylie and she just shrugs. We start walking down to the field. Before we get all the way down the whole football team comes running out holding signs. I stop in front of the bleachers and look at them like they are all crazy. "Mom me and Dad have to show you something." Kegan smiles and steps forward. The boys start flipping the signs over that they are holding.   WILL. YOU. MARRY. And at the end of the line is Danny down on one knee. I run out on the field and Danny grabs me and hugs me. "Baby I know things haven't always been right but you are my home. You and Kegan are all I ever wanted. I messed up the past and I can't fix that. But I can fix the future and I want to have that future with you and my son. Jas will you marry me?" Danny asks softly with tears in his eyes.   "Your are The Promise Danny. So, Yes, Yes I will marry you."

The End

ABOUT THE AUTHOR

L.T. Kenneth was born and raised in a small township named Botshabelo in South Africa, where he also studied in the local schools of his born town. He then began his relish passion of writing fiction from his early teen, which changed his life around. After publishing short-stories through small publications, he began writing novels because of the reception for his paranormal romance stories. Which he still writes today.

COMING SOON.
1. The Titanium (Destiny of Love part 2 and 3)
2. The Titanium (Gift of Love part 1,2 and 3)
3. The Titanium (Awe of Love part 1,2, and 3

The Promise

www.ingramcontent.com/pod-product-compliance
Lightning Source LLC
Chambersburg PA
CBHW070354130626
46556CB00007B/3165